We Write the North

We Write the North

*An Anthology of New Work
from The Writing Squad*

THE WRITING SQUAD

Published in 2023 by The Writing Squad
11 Weston Grove
Stockport
SK4 5DW
www.writingsquad.com

ISBN 978-1-7390997-1-8

Foreword © Angelique Tran Van Sang
Text © The Contributors 2023
The moral rights of the authors have been asserted.

Cataloguing-in-Publication Data
A catalogue record for this book is available from the British Library.

All rights reserved. No part of this publication may be reproduced or transmitted in any form or by any means, electronic or mechanical, including photocopying, recording or any other information storage or retrieval system, without prior permission in writing from the publisher.

Edited by Marigold Atkey
Jacket Artwork by Emma Ewbank
Book design and typesetting by Laura Jones-Rivera
and Katie McLean
Printed in UK by Biddles

The Writing Squad gratefully acknowledges the support of
Arts Council England.

Contents

Foreword | Angelique Tran Van Sang — vii

Her Strange Addiction | *Isabella Sharp* — 1
Wishbone | *Emily Yates* — 11
The Littoral Line | *Alice Noel* — 23
Made for Two | *James Varney* — 29
The Clocks Change | *Beth Lee* — 33
Reverie | *Jenny Metcalfe* — 45
Words Spoken Over a Bleeding Warrior |
   Finlay Worrallo — 57
Round Trip | *Vivienne Burgess* — 65
Bringing Home | *Lauren C. Maltas* — 75
Under Red Light | *Rory Thorp* — 83

Contributor Biographies — 97
Acknowledgements — 95

Foreword

When Steve Dearden first approached me about creating an anthology for The Writing Squad, I didn't hesitate. I first encountered the work of the Squad when I was an editor, and the publisher I worked for held an introductory day for Squad members, to teach them about the publication process. Steve had sent through the work of several Squad members to the editorial team beforehand. If I'm honest, I hadn't expected anything to come from the day, given these were unagented writers, early in their careers. More fool me. I was blindsided by a handful of stories from one author, that were completely fresh and unexpected – with a strength of voice and perspective that I hadn't encountered before. I put them in touch with an agent, and said I wanted to publish them, no matter what – I had that much confidence in what I had read. Those stories formed what would become *Send Nudes*, a now multi-award winning collection by the writer Saba Sams, a Granta Best of Young British Novelist.

I'm telling this story not just to explain the quality of writing by the Squad members, but also to emphasise the importance of the existence of the Squad to the ecosystem of publishing in the UK. Writers are not born – at least, not in my opinion. To me, writing is a craft learned through practice. Talent is important, but it needs nurturing, encouragement, support, and perhaps most crucially, the time, space and permission to experiment, to find a voice of one's own. But the opportunities to do so are few and far between, particularly outside of London and major cities, and especially for those who do not have the financial means, or traditional pathways to follow. This is where the work of the Squad comes in.

Working with all genres – poets and prose writers, playwrights and script writers, creative-non fictioneers, lyricists and performance artists, as well as those who want to try everything, and those who haven't decided if or what they want to specialise in, The Writing Squad provides a free two-year programme of workshops and 1-1 support for writers aged 16-22 who live, work or study in the North of England. After those two years, they continue to support writers as they begin their careers.

What you'll find in these pages is the result of a call-out last year for writers to contribute a story to an anthology that summarises the work of The Writing Squad today. There was a word limit, but no other restrictions. Along with my fellow judges Lauren Whybrow and Madeleine

Feeny, we whittled the submissions down to a top ten, which was passed on to Daunt Books Publisher Marigold Atkey for editorial input.

Our robust discussions about the stories made for a rousing evening. We passionately put forth arguments for our favourites, clashing only a few times (we all remain friends). Though we had to make hard decisions, we are satisfied with the wide range – from a surreal horror-inflected story of consumerism both literal and metaphorical (Her Strange Addiction), to a tender tale of intergenerational rituals (Wishbone); a disarmingly understated story of climate-woe (The Littoral Line) to a fleeting but powerful exploration of bodies (Made for Two); an uncanny meditation on time management (The Clocks Change) to a gently hopeful story of class and classical music (Reverie); a dogged revenge story with an unexpected twist (Words Spoken Over a Bleeding Warrior) to a haunting bus ride (Round Trip); a near-miss accident that exposes what we misunderstand in each other (Bringing Home) to a story of alienation and release abroad (Under Red Light).

There is so much talent here – and in the end, there was no satisfactory way I could summarise what defined these writers, beyond an exciting breadth of work. These are just talented writers, at the beginning of their careers, with all the world ahead. I hope you enjoy.

Angelique Tran Van Sang

HER STRANGE ADDICTION

Isabella Sharp

'Is that birthday cake for the whole floor, or just the department, do you think?'

Sadie had been staring over at the handbag department, hoping to make them feel uncomfortable as they clustered around the cake. It was a novelty one, shaped like a handbag. She spent a lot of her time at work thinking about food. She worked on the perfume counter, which meant that her nose and sinuses were chemically blown out by the end of her shift. It caused her tastebuds to jangle in anticipation every time she sprayed a fragrance, but by the end of the day her hunger had evaporated. She would still eat once she was home but the parosmia always lingered, turning steaks and asparagus and salmon into one flavourless medium with textural differences. She turned her head to face Helen from the skincare counter.

'Department, it looks like.'

'Cunts,' said Helen, then smiled at a customer who was coming down the escalator. From Sadie's experience, she knew sound travelled strangely in the shop. The hum of the air conditioning and the position of the speakers meant that there were dead spots, like the escalator, and others where it was easy to be overheard, like the tills. 'How can I help you today?' Helen said to the approaching customer, her voice going up one bright octave, as she left to show the woman their new releases. Sadie listened to her tell the customer about moisture barriers and the benefits of humectants.

The handbag manager drew out a long knife and sank it into the cake. The other employees held paper towels and it made Sadie think of school assemblies. She gazed out across the doldrums of the shop. The escalators moved, carrying nothing and no-one up and down. Overhead was a tinted glass dome showing a swollen January sky. Rain was hitting it with force but the tinny music echoing around the place made it inaudible. Sadie had once had stitches on her foot and watched with interest as the sides of the wound were pulled together, able only to feel a faint tugging, thanks to a local anaesthetic injection. This was much like that. She checked the till clock, which was 23 minutes slow, and decided to take her break early.

'Helen, can you cover my counter?'

Helen looked up from where she was smearing a customer's cheek with face cream.

'If you give me the earlier afternoon break.'

'Fine.'

Sadie went to the food hall to eat at the discounted sushi counter. The place sucked all her wages out of her, transformed into gloves or lipstick, leaving her with a disconcerting yawn of overdraft. She found Celine from men's accessories already sitting there. Celine sold menswear easily. She would lean forward, tilt her head to the side and engage unsuspecting men in conversation in order to probe at their emotional fractures. Like the cool fingers of a doctor on a swollen ankle, pressing to form an inverted image of the joint, she would calmly assess the situation and offer them solace in luxury goods.

After lunch, Sadie sold one item in six hours. She was working a late shift and was there long after most of the others had left. The only available exit was down the shadowy hall of the rare handbag exhibition. The building was Victorian, and the rare handbag exhibition was tiled. Her footsteps echoed as she passed by the glass cases. It reminded her of a natural history museum. Various endangered animals had been skinned and moulded into receptacles which now sat under halogen lights to protect them from fingerprints and theft.

The material was too valuable to be pierced by security tags, so they had tags looped around their handles and attached to systems within the plinths like a life support system. The overhead lights were off, so the material glistened under the display lights as if it were alive. She paused by the last bag, a snowy lizard Birkin, and stared. Perhaps it had been the long day and lack of stimulation, but she felt sure that if she bit into it that it would taste good. Like soft, bland cheese. When she was a baby and not breastfeeding properly she had been underweight. The midwife had recommended feeding her spoonfuls of calorie-rich mascarpone to increase her weight.

'You heading out?'

The security guard was waiting by the door, expectant. She nodded and smiled, slipped out into the night and slept dreamlessly in her shoebox apartment. In the morning, she made eggs with high-protein yogurt whipped into them. When she ate them, they tasted like polystyrene. She scraped her plate into the bin, took some medication left over from last year's winter sickness bug, and got ready for work. She wore a black suit with a creamy wash of eyeshadow called *Guilty Pleasure* that her manager had made a passive-aggressive comment about the previous week, telling her that she looked tired.

When she went into work, she stopped to inspect the new window display. It was jungle themed. The expanse of glass was bristling with plants, forming a dense wall of foliage. The purpose was to celebrate a new ornamental collection, a collaboration between Cartier and Bulgari. An enterprising window assistant had clipped watches around the limbs of a bamboo at alternating levels, a light angled from above to pick out their leather straps. Sadie had a clipping from a crocodile plant which she was propagating in the humid air of her bathroom at home. It was suffering and she did not know what to do with it.

She was waylaid by Danny close to the escalators. A wiry security guard in his early forties, Danny would appear normal on first impression, until he began to drip-feed his habit of asking questions for the purpose of cutting you off in order to tell you his own opinions. He seemed to think she was younger than her actual age and liked to educate her about things which she already knew.

'Morning,' Danny said, aggressively.

'Hello.'

'Quiet one, today,' he said, and put his hands behind his back, rocked on the balls of his feet. 'What you reading?' he asked, seizing on the book poking out of her bag.

'A novel. It's about the trial of the most sophisticated catfish case in the UK—'

'Good, good,' he said, his eyes sliding away from her. 'Good for you, reading. Make sure you do it, you hear me?'

It rankled with her, his paternal, chiding tone. Customers loved him because he would joke with children; wag his finger at them for letting go of their balloons.

'Bye, Danny.'

He waved her off and went back to prowling an empty store for shoplifters. Sadie rose like Christ up the escalator and went to her counter where she began the comforting scratch of daily sales figures. By mid-morning there was a dryness in her throat and an itch which would not go away. She drank more water than usual and at lunch she ordered hot spiced noodle soup in the hope that it would flush out her sinuses. It got worse. She felt the characteristic tickle of a post-nasal drip and resigned herself to sleeping propped up by pillows that night. She went into the women's bathroom for a coughing fit, sat on the closed toilet lid. On the back of the stall doors a much-loathed shop designer had decided to print bracing slogans with messages like *perfection is persistence*. In her stall, the original message had been vandalised. All that remained was a nonsensical pile of vowels, spelling a disjointed cousin of *help* out of the remaining letters, *holpess.*

That night she had no desire to eat. She finished her shift and stumbled out through the handbag gallery, coughing as she went. In the car park, she hunched over in the driver's seat of her vehicle, coughing until she felt something foreign in the back of her throat, bumping against her tonsils. She gagged and reached into her mouth; she could not re-swallow the object. She tilted her head back to open her airway, and her fingers found purchase on something; she pulled and felt the odd sensation of an object moving up her oesophagus. When she pulled again it came out in a wet string, a strand of parma ham fat, slapped wetly against her cheek like a man operating his dick in porn. She examined it. It was a single, filmy stocking.

She drove home, took off her makeup, and went to sleep. In the morning she was convinced she had imagined the whole thing. She went back into work and nodded as her manager talked her through a new product launch. She tried to ignore a persistent itch on the inner skin of her right knee. It began to prickle like a heat rash as the day went on. She had intermittent dermatitis, triggered by washing powders. She chalked it up to that. When she went to the toilet, she yanked down her tights and began to scratch, only to stop dead when she felt a new lump of uneven skin. Once in a fitness phase she had used a foam roller, pulping her leg muscles with it to stimulate recovery and blood flow. In the morning she had woken up, thrown away the duvets and reeled back in shock from the dark brown splotches that had bloomed like spores on her skin overnight. They hadn't hurt; she wondered if she had been bitten or assaulted, before she remembered the foam roller and was able to relax, her heartrate subsiding.

In the cubicle, she gritted her teeth and looked at her leg. The colour of the skin was unblemished. She ran her fingers over it, testing. There seemed to be a ring of hard unyielding flesh under the skin, possibly a cyst or a lipoma. She remembered walking past the jewellery counter the day before, when the store associates were behaving like a flock of hens facing live-shackle slaughter, asking if anyone had sold a bangle encrusted with diamonds. Sadie always thought it was ugly. She'd stopped and stared at the glass case, unnoticed, and looked at the white velour where the bracelet usually sat, moulded to keep it snugly in place. It was empty now. In the toilet cubicle, Sadie pulled up her tights again and rearranged her clothes, before returning to the shop floor.

That evening she looked up videos of minor surgery on Youtube and went to a late-opening pharmacy for a collection of items: a craft knife, iodine, numbing cream and bandages. She propped up her leg and smoothed the cream over the skin until she could poke it with tweezers and feel nothing. Then she flicked a lighter and ran it over the craft knife to sanitise it, waited for it to cool. Then she used the craft knife and the tweezers to make a small, deep incision, cleaning away the blood absent-mindedly with an alcohol wipe. She delved into the dark weep of the wound with the tweezers until she gained purchase on the object nestled inside, wincing when she pushed too deep and felt the muscle of her own body. She pulled out a bracelet in a bloody string, as though it were a parasite, and put it into a bowl. She applied butterfly stitches to the wound and elevated her leg until the blood clotted, scrolling through videos on her phone. She looked at a dark video of a woman in a room, removing an abscess on her boyfriend's back by poking a needle through the eruption, before hooking out the caul of the cyst sack with gloved fingers. She came across a video of a haunch of recently butchered beef. The flesh twitched and rippled as the muscle cells died, disturbingly lifelike. She decided to take meat off her shopping list that week.

More objects began to surface in different orifices and planes of her body. In April, she found another stocking curled tight as a snail shell within her inner ear canal. Later that month, she traced the outline of a pair of sunglasses below the taut skin of her hipbone. Her food bills dwindled to nothing. She did not remember how her change in diet started, much like adults would not remember their transition from pureed to solid food as a baby, but the objects she particularly liked or disliked were marked out. A logo-stamped purse did not agree with her; she brought up garbled phrases all day like bad gas and had to hide her mouth in the crook of her elbow to expel them, pretending she had a cough.

She found a favourite the first time she crunched down a plastic bottle of skin serum; the texture was reminiscent of a cooked prawn tail, the soft burst of the goo inside like tapioca. Fusion food! Time went on. She passed through the doors of the department store unchallenged, concealing a trove of objects veiled within her body, their taste lingering on the zones of her tongue. Leather was bitter. Face cream was sweet, like mascarpone. Now and again, she wore the bracelet she had fished out of her knee when she socialised with people outside of work, and when they asked her where she'd got it, she smiled.

WISHBONE

Emily Yates

The chicken was slimy.

Josie shrieked and scrubbed her hands against her thighs.

Grandma whipped out a towel. 'Don't wipe your hands on your trousers.'

Pinching her lips together, Josie shook her head. 'I don't like the chicken.'

'The chicken doesn't like you.'

'Why?' She crossed her arms.

Crunching salt and pepper onto the chicken, Grandma said, 'If you're going to stay in the kitchen, get me the butter.'

Josie opened the fridge with both hands. 'Why doesn't the chicken like me?'

Cutting up the butter, Grandma arranged it around the tray. 'You're about to eat her. Would you want to be eaten?'

She placed the chicken in the oven. A wave of heat singed Josie's cheeks. Grandma began peeling the potatoes.

'No,' Josie said, arranging the scraps of skin into a smiley face. And then a sad one. She jumped up to sit on the counter, legs swinging back and forth. 'Did you kill the chicken yourself?' She could imagine it: the quiet snap of the bird's neck, Grandma's flint stare and her cane scraping against the barn floor as she left.

'Your father did it.'

Josie's stomach was turned over like soil. 'Does it hurt?'

'Only for a second.'

'Like a pinch of pain?'

Grandma dropped the potatoes into a pan. 'Just a pinch.'

Josie's chin dripped with meat juice.

Grandma watched her, spine of oak in the oak chair. She cut the broccoli carefully, chewed each bite slowly. 'Take your time, Josie.'

Carving a slice of chicken, Josie imitated her grandma. 'When will Dad eat?' Words and food tangled.

'Don't talk while you eat. He'll be back from the dairy soon.'

Josie didn't speak for the rest of the meal. She felt the silence around her, like sheep's wool. Wiping her mouth on her napkin, she asked, 'What happens to the rest of the chicken?'

Picking up her plate, Grandma said, 'I cut off the rest of the meat and boil the bones for broth.'

Josie tried not to pull a face.

'Broth is good for you.' Grandma clomped back into the kitchen.

Following her like a gnat, Josie watched her grandma as she pulled apart the bird, separating bones into one bowl and meat into another. She set something aside.

Josie crept closer. 'What's that?'

'A wishbone.'

'You can make a wish?' Josie held both ribs between her fingers. 'How?'

Taking it from her, Grandma put the wishbone on the windowsill and said, 'Ask me in a week.'

Josie checked on the wishbone every morning before school.

Sometimes, she crawled out of bed and looked at it when the moon hung in the window like a button. It spun in the sky over the week, full to waning.

The cockerel shrieked Josie out of her dream. After stuffing her feet into her slippers, she crept down the stairs. The kitchen was a graveyard of cabinets and morning shadows and Grandma's ghost. Josie glanced at the doorway before climbing onto the counter. On the windowsill, the wishbone had turned chalky white;

Josie wanted to draw along the walls with its delicate tips.

She didn't touch it.

Grandma's cane knocked against the hallway floor.

Leaping off the counter, Josie put some bread into the toaster.

Grandma stopped in the doorway. 'Don't walk around in the dark.'

'But I had carrots last night. Dad says they make you see in the dark,' Josie said, warming her hands above the toaster. 'Like a cat. He says we might get a cat, too.'

Grandma remained silent as she pushed towards the windowsill. 'It's ready.'

Josie wanted to shriek like the cockerel. Her toes curled up. 'What do we do?'

Pinching one rib of the wishbone, Grandma offered the other to Josie. 'Pull.'

It snapped.

Grandma held up the spine. 'I get the wish.'

'Why?' Josie was snapped in two.

'My part stayed in one piece.'

'So I don't get a wish?'

Turning on the kitchen light, Grandma said, 'Not this time.'

Josie's toast had burned.

Grandma didn't cook another chicken for two weeks.

Josie fought through beef brisket and smoked mackerel and lamb chops. She waited, hovered in the doorway each time Grandma started cooking.

On the fifteenth day, Josie ran from her bus stop to the farm gate. Grandma was plucking a dead chicken in the yard.

'Is it for dinner?'

Grandma didn't look up. She was a machine, skin cracked like the paint on the tractor. Dad said they needed a new one. 'Roast dinner,' she replied.

Wish dinner, Josie thought.

There was a new wishbone in the window.

Josie traced the ribs with her eyes. She wanted to touch it, but she didn't want to ruin the wish.

Her hands burned above the toaster. Turning it off, she rescued the blackened bread.

Knocking along the hallway, Grandma said, 'The wishbone won't dry up any quicker if you watch it.'

Josie buried her head in her toast as she spread jam over it. 'I'm not watching it.'

'There are other ways to make wishes.' The teacups clattered as Grandma grabbed one, the kettle whispering.

Licking the jam off her fingers, Josie asked, 'Like how?'

'My mother used to bury things.'

'What things?' Josie felt like the electric fence around the pig enclosure.

Shoulders lifting, hands tightening around her mug, Grandma said, 'Things she liked. She believed that the earth would grant a wish if you gave up something valuable. She buried her wedding ring after my father died.' Grandma looked out of the window, at the barn, at the sheep disappearing over the hill. 'I've not seen it since.'

'She sounds crazy.'

'Don't be rude.'

Josie scurried up the stairs.

Grandma was sitting in her chair.

From the doorway, Josie could see the back of her head, the fire haloing it. Josie had once asked why she sat there, doing nothing. Grandma had said, 'I like to think.'

Josie never asked what she thought about. Instead, she ran off to name the chickens again.

'What do you want?' Grandma asked.

Josie was a vegetable pulled from the earth, exposed. 'Nothing.'

'Don't hover, then.'

Josie stayed in the doorway. 'Can I bury something?'

'I don't know, can you?'

'I don't know how to.' Taking a step into the living room, Josie asked, 'Can you show me how?'

'What do you have to bury?' Grandma creaked to standing.

Holding out her hands from behind her back, Josie presented a pinecone, silver glitter glued along its honeycomb edges. 'I made it in school.'

Inspecting it, Grandma said, 'Very good. The earth will love this.'

Josie leaped to the garden, Grandma on her shadow. The cold was pinching, and so Josie hopped on the spot. 'Where do we bury it?'

Grandma surveyed the field. 'Beside the broken wall.'

They stumbled through the wind, Josie leading Grandma around where the giants had scooped out palmfuls of land and dumped them to the side. That's what Dad said: 'They used to live in the trees across the road. Our land – before it was our land – was their playground.'

'Did you ever see the giants?' Josie asked.

Grandma had pulled her jumper to her nose. 'What giants?'

'The ones who played here,' she said, pointing at a hole in the field.

Grandma squinted at it. 'I was born after they left.'

'Where did they go?'

'Back into the caves under the forest. They're sleeping.'

Josie went to ask another question, but Grandma stopped before the broken wall. 'Here.'

The stones were crumbling. Josie imagined a giant tripping over and landing on them.

'Did you bring anything to dig with?' Grandma asked.

Clutching the pinecone to her chest, Josie said, 'No.'

'You'll have to use your hands, then.'

Grandma leant against the wall, eyes closed, while Josie dug. As her fingers ate away at the earth, she grinned. The pinecone lay in its grave and she covered it up. 'What do I do now?'

'Say your wish out loud.'

'I wish that the giants wake up and play a game of football in the garden with me.'

Grandma nodded. 'Let's go.'

The next day, Josie woke up and pulled open her curtains. The giants were still asleep. She slouched downstairs and checked on the wishbone. It was almost dry.

'I think the giants left a message for you outside,' Grandma shouted from the stairs.

Slinging down the arm of the toaster, Josie ran into the garden. A bedsheet hung on the washing line, and a message had been painted on it with dirt. '*We giants are too big and clumsy to play football but thank you for inviting us.*'

She jumped in a circle.

From the window, Grandma read the note. Then, 'Come back inside,' she called. 'You'll catch a cold.'

The moon had almost finished its pirouette by the time they broke the wishbone.

Grandma won again.

'Why do you always win?' Josie bit out.

Grandma took a seat at the dinner table. 'Maybe I need the wish more than you.'

'What did you wish for?'

She took a drink of her tea. 'Go and get ready for school.'

They agreed to pull only one wishbone and make only one burial every month.

Grandma would win the wishbone, and Josie would bury something: a picture she drew, her favourite bauble, the last sweet in her bag. She said her wish out loud. Grandma kept hers silent, stored in a jar with the other wishbones, snapped and unsnapped.

Josie wished for new mittens, and they appeared on the dinner table.

She wished for a cat and a framed picture of one was hung in her room.

She wished for a holiday, and summer transformed the garden into Eden.

Josie opened her birthday presents and kept aside one of her doll's new outfits.

Gathering the wrapping paper, Grandma spied the dress in Josie's hands. 'Are you going to bury that?'

They went out into the garden together and buried it underneath the oak tree. Josie wished for another dress for her doll.

Sometimes, Josie would follow a trail around the garden. She started at the broken wall and wove through the sheep field to the trough, where she'd buried a pair of socks, then over to a giant's footprint, a picture book buried beneath it.

The walk took forty minutes to complete. She timed herself.

Grandma always had a cup of tea waiting for her once she got back.

The rules changed: only one wishbone, on Christmas Day, and only two burials a year. Grandma said that the earth could only hold a finite number of wishes.

Josie turned eleven and she wished for rollerblades. She joined a club and raced every Tuesday.

The next year she wished for straight teeth. She chose the purple braces.

When she was thirteen, she wished for a boyfriend. 'Philip is a very nice boy,' Grandma said one day. 'Why don't you invite him round for dinner?'

Grandma started to stoke the fire hotter, and cut her chicken into smaller pieces, leaving half of them. Her skin became thinner and colder.

Josie danced around her, with more stories of more people she'd met at school, more inches on her legs.

They cooked together. Josie did the whisking and grabbed the spices from the top shelf. She filled the kettle whenever Grandma said, 'I'm going to make a cup of tea.'

The jar of wishbones, both wished and waiting, was almost full.

There was a new one drying in the window.

Josie poured out her cereal and watched the wishbone while she chewed.

Grandma didn't come downstairs.

Dumping the bowl in the sink, Josie ran up to her bedroom and grabbed her schoolbag. She knocked on Grandma's door. 'Are you alright?'

The cockerel howled.

Josie tried to pretend that Grandma had gone to sleep like the giants, but it didn't work.

Grandma hadn't ever cried, and Josie never did in front of her. So, she didn't cry now, not in the kitchen, not in front of the wishbone jar. Crying was reserved for the shower and under her duvet.

Josie cooked a chicken.

She diced the butter and used too much pepper. She went for another shower while it cooked.

The chicken was still hot as she pulled it apart, meat in one bowl and bones in another. She found the wishbone, held it like glass.

The wishbone dried in the winter sun quicker than usual.

Josie pulled on her grandma's woolly coat of armour. Grabbing the new wishbone and the jar from the windowsill, she walked into the garden.

She knelt, rain soaking through her trousers, and dug another hole beside the broken wall. Her hands created a cave, but there were no giants within. She placed the jar inside. She broke the new wishbone and held the winning rib in her left hand. Laying it on top of the jar, Josie buried it all.

THE LITTORAL LINE

Alice Noel

The shed had been teetering for weeks now, maybe months – only took a bout or so of bad weather and boom, it was gone.

Don't get me wrong, I knew the cliff was a risk when we moved back. Been watching that coastline inch closer since I was a kid, not that I paid much attention then. Kids don't to that kind of stuff, do they? They'd rather be chucking cow pat-covered sticks at each other. Mine would, anyway. But we were sensible, researched the maps and the satellite shots. Hell, I even read papers with graphs and erosion rates.

We'll have a couple of years here, at least. By then, I reckon they'll have done something about the cliffs – there's always some new technology springing up. It's amazing how they can break all this stuff down these days. My parents didn't have that. They'd never have known. All they wanted was a family home by the sea. Probably best that they didn't see the cliff crumble closer, never mind their bloody shed drop off the edge.

That's why we came back here after I inherited, despite the council letters. I couldn't see someone else move into my parents' house, redecorate and add hotchpotch extensions. Come to think of it, they'd never have got the planning permission. Stick one JCB anywhere near that edge and all you'll end up with is a pile of yellow scrap. No, we were planning to sell – I helped the estate agents give the tour, a bit of family insight into the home, you know? Thought I could drum up interest, maybe help people overlook the facts a bit. The house itself is beautiful. Spacious, plenty of cosy nooks for the winter; loads of great hiding places – providing you don't get stuck, that is.

I did, once. Got locked in the shed out there. Rain hammering down and the waves having a party below. Nowadays the whole house shudders in weather like that. At least the sea was a bit further away back then. I thought the world was going to end. The latch caught from the outside when I went in, can't remember what for. I shouted myself hoarse, a waste of vocal cords. No one came looking. My brother must have told them I'd already gone to bed. He always was a wind-up. I spent the night cowering in the corner thinking I was done for – Dad's tools were rattling and all I could find to sit on were a couple of kneeling mats. Never been able to look at a hoe the same way since. Mum discovered me in the morning when she needed some string to tie her climbers back up. Anyway, it's gone now. They all are.

None of the viewers were interested in that. Most asked how long the walk was from door to beach. They wanted somewhere they could come in the summer that didn't stink of grease and petrol, I expect. I told them about the chippy down the road – how when the wind's right you get the smell of freshly cut potato and frying batter wafting over – but sea grease isn't the same as city grease. It's the salt in the air, see? Makes everything feel fresh.

None of those pillocks would have loved this place like she deserves.

A lot of people are selling up round here now. Not too surprising – they want to be able to get away before they're completely out of pocket. You probably saw the signs as you drove in. Or trying to sell, I should say. The only real estate going now is in the wind farms. Still, the work caused a lot of upset. People complaining about the view being spoilt when the turbines don't produce much – even if half the year you can hardly see out that far. The kids like watching them, though. They've been told they'll get to go up one next year at school. On dry land, thank god. Dread to think what the health and safety forms would be like.

My dad would never have been bothered with all that. If you broke a bone doing something, it was a lesson learned; if you got worse than that then you were downright stupid in his books. Take the incident with the shed. I came in crying – I was only eight – and he told me if I had been that scared, I'd have worked out how to use one of the trowels to break the lock open. Didn't get much sympathy there. He spent more time in the garden than the house. Don't get me wrong, he was there for the big moments, if you had a prize to collect or something. Though that was more my brother than me. He loved us though, I know he did.

I don't remember feeling cut off out here when I was small – the fields felt wild, but never isolated. It makes you worry for the old dears down in the village; some of them don't have family left, or none they talk to. If something goes tits up, who are they going to call? We don't get thick snow here, driest county and all – not to mention the milder winters. I try to check in with them when I can. A couple of them were old even when I was a kid. Got to keep that community going while the village is still there.

That's where the veg patches used to be – where those rocks jut out. Careful, a step too far and you'll be in them. No coming back from that; not even the lifeguards could save you. Course, I cleared the beds out before the land went. We'd had good use of them:

potatoes, tomatoes, French beans, radishes. You name it, we grew it. Or tried to – some came out better than others. The carrots were a disaster; so black with fly you'd never have thought they were meant to be orange. Last year we found the seed packet. Turns out they were a purple variety.

It wasn't too much of a wrench, seeing those beds go. The sleepers were pretty old and split – not surprising if you think how they've been there thirty years since my dad laid them. I don't think he ever fixed them after my brother and I put a dent in the wood with a wheelbarrow when we were playing some silly game. He was funny like that – if you left the milk out of the fridge he'd rant for hours but break a fence panel and he'd shrug it off. Mum wouldn't. She used to keep roses in pots up on the patio there, the soil's too sandy for proper borders. If a ball got too close, we were chucked out into the lane to find somewhere else to play. No shortage of space for that round here, though.

You didn't have to watch out on the sand so much, then. The bricks and nails have built up over the years. We don't let the kids run around bare foot down there anymore. Last summer there was a nasty incident where a dog ended up with a nail through its paw. The owner put in a complaint to the council – we've heard nothing since. There are plenty of warning signs around. Some argue too many. You still find people setting up camp right below the cliffs, even though you can see the old water pipes sticking out of the clay higher up.

We have the same problem with the tide warnings you get further round the coast; lifeguards have to rescue idiots every year. Not much of an issue on this stretch – lucky really, considering we lost the lifeboat station several years back. The danger is when the tide whips in. If you're watching the water properly you see it coming, but there are whole stretches of sand that get cut off pretty quickly. From the beach huts you can see the poor sods, a bit like some kind of modern art sculpture until they start waving and you realise it's time to call the coastguard.

The shed seems like a big deal, but I reckon we'll be okay. The house will last. Other people are selling up even though there's time – they're trying new measures down on the beach. New gabions and that, although at this point the defences are more to stop the rubble from battering down the cliffs in the heavier weather. People don't want to move out to communities like this anymore. They want the convenience of the big supermarkets and suburban life. The one café has to shut up shop out of season – there aren't enough customers in the winter months. Same with community centres, churches, libraries. It's a ghost town round here. Sometimes feels like we're at the bottom of the sea already, if you ask me.

We'll be fine, I'm sure. We'll be fine.

MADE FOR TWO

James Varney

there is no more perfect way to measure the presence of my body in the world than this. more exact than the shadow portraits you made of me in our first winter together. I remove my swim trunks feeling silly to have kept them on this far. the water I displace is my shadow. you stand opposite at the brim of your own tank. our bare bodies so familiar to each other are alien within this steel room and under the eyes of the surgical team. when we tread into our twin basins we move together. water the temperature of blood fills my ears and nostrils and covers my eyes and I think *we have it. we have it.*

we have anxious questions first. we research and trace the journeys of others who have taken this path. we understand the risks and we know the work of the surgeons cannot be undone. this is what we want. but still we ask our questions which begin with an *uh* an *ih* an *oh*. my mind puddles with doubts about the procedure and this decision we have made. then you ask *will it be warm?* and I look over at your bright face which light shines out of and I think *yes. yes of course it will be warm*.

in the days before today we test *us* and *we* when before *you* and *I* would have marked the air between us. one day we hold hands the whole eighteen hours we are awake. the skin of our palms is clammy and safe. we share sweat, pronouns, everything.

love is a story we tell ourselves. we make our own language for it. when I tell my family they do not want me to explain. they do not want to understand the ways they have not known me for years and perhaps my entire life. I am unwell they tell me. they blame you as I knew they would. when they ask if they can visit us I tell the truth that they would not recognise us. they can if they want. you will be gone forever they say and I tell them I know. get married they say not knowing that marriage is only a contract and I could not love a contract. I can love our body in the way I love yours. I can love our body in the way I love our life. you are not making me do this I try to explain to them. their answers are only noises. they don't know how to talk to me and I think they never did.

the surgeons will knit our two bodies and their sound minds together. we will wake in a single flesh with a hard conical shell. we will survive drought. we will suck in stained air and water and pass it back into the world clean. we will move only slowly and grow slower. we will build our body from sand and we will feed on what the world passes by. we give our whole selves to each other and the world and the sea.

when we are introduced to our shell it is smaller than we expected. without our bones we will be smaller too. a body is mostly water and water fills the container you give it. you will grow they tell us. they do not know how long we will live but that is unimportant to us. our time will be measured in tides. we walk to the site where we will wake tomorrow. how strange, to have legs, to have four feet instead of one. there is a view of the sea but we will not have eyes. we will feel it in our flesh. its nearby pulse will sing to us of welcome salt. we crest the stones before the beach and *oh*. you say it has hit you that this is our home now that the song of the breaking waves is our life now that this is it for ever.

of those who have transformed none have reported back. they must be content. they were as sure as we are and we will be as happy as them. this is the bravest and the strongest we have been. this conviction is the love we have together and stronger because we do not only have love we are love and that is what we are becoming. we are becoming love. I read these words to you before we go under. the anaesthetist is at hand and waits patiently with his needles and tubes knowing exactly how we weigh knowing our metabolisms and how they will reply to his art. this is the last time we will be two. the last time we are awake in our separate bodies. we are ready. we have rehearsed our answers and the world of blades closes in on us this final time and we are ready with our last words. *yes. yes I do. yes I understand. I am. we do. we are.*

THE CLOCKS CHANGE

Beth Lee

He squeezed my toes through the blanket.

'Your alarm clock's still broken.'

He was standing over the edge of my bed, dripping. His form was dark and fuzzy, just like in my paralysis dreams. But unlike in my dreams, I found my voice to speak.

'I'll get a new one.'

He took the towel from around his waist, dropped it on the bed and started to put on his uniform, which was scattered across the floor. I was surprised he could distinguish anything in the early morning grey. He leaned over and kissed me and his lips were wet and cold. He smelled of the lime shower gel I kept for him and the aftershave he'd buy buckets of when he came through customs.

'I'll probably see you next week,' he said. 'Fix the clock. You know I keep a tight schedule.'

He grabbed the bag he'd never unpacked from the chair and left.

Daniel was a flight attendant and had a tendency to take off. He was the plane and I was the turbulence he hit every so often. This was the first time he'd visited my new flat since I'd moved in a month ago. I'd rented the place even though it was just out of my budget – it was a good size and location for us if he ever changed his mind and moved in.

I slipped out of bed and scooped up his wet towel. In the kitchen, the curtains were still open. Two tall windows let in the first cool light of the spring day, making the tiled floor look like a deep lake I didn't want to tread across. I hung the towel on the rack in the bathroom and went back to bed, falling asleep to the sound of a drunkard smashing glass on the street.

As soon as I woke up I knew that I'd overslept. Daniel was right to criticise my clock – the alarm hadn't gone off. Light reached its long arms around the curtains as if to shake my shoulder and tell me I was late. I turned my phone over. It was already 9:30 a.m. I hurriedly changed and ran out the door.

I hadn't moved far from my old flat, but it made sense to take a different way to work. I'd already walked the new route a few times, but this time I noticed a shop I'd never seen before. A smiling old man watched me through the window while he wound up a clock. The shelves in the window were lined with clocks – large, small, retro, antique – and each showed exactly the same time. Even the seconds seemed to be ticking in unison. I smiled back but he had slipped out of sight.

I hurried through the automatic doors into work and immediately knocked into a mannequin, catching it before it fell. I couldn't get it to stand straight, so I carried it under my arm to the counter where I could see my manager.

'I told you before this doesn't work,' I said. 'There's no space for the mannequin at the front, people walk into it all the time.'

Her eyes went past me and her hands busied themselves removing a sticker from a label.

'You can lecture me when you show up on time,' she said.

She never wanted to listen. I'd already worked there for five years and I knew how everything should be laid out. I knew that putting the brighter clothes in the window dissuaded our usual customers, that there was never enough space for the sale items if they were put in the alcove, that there should always be someone lingering around the shop floor in case someone had a question, instead of in the back room on their phone.

She told me to return the mannequin and I complied, not caring to tuck its blouse back into its trousers.

On my way home I passed the clock shop again, but it was closed. Nearly all the clocks were showing the wrong time. I peeked through the glass to see if the man was there, but couldn't spot him. It must be so easy for clocks to go completely wrong, and then what use did they have? If the mechanism was off by just a little, it could fall out of time so quickly. Did the man have to reset them every single morning so no one noticed?

There was one alarm clock on the top shelf that caught my eye. It was modern looking, with large digits ticking down, in a sleek chrome casing. It was exactly the kind Daniel would like. He always went on about design, how style should be about simplicity and elegance.

I made a habit of checking the clocks each time I passed, so that by the end of the week I'd memorised the entire shopfront. Only three clocks maintained the right time, all the rest seemed to pick whatever time they liked.

After about a week had passed, as I approached the shop, I could sense something was wrong. Some of the clocks had changed. The yellow, 1960s-style alarm clock was now twice as wide. The plastic had expanded to incase it, like acid-yellow lava. One clock face, which had once had a monogram, now had an image of a bird. The hands of another were now in an ornate, dagger shape.

I stepped back and scrutinised each clock, looking for other changes, and when I couldn't find anything else I took a picture on my phone and hurried to work. Every spare moment possible, I looked at the photo under the counter. I could only see those three differences, but I could feel that there were more. The arrangement wasn't quite right, or maybe some had altered size just slightly. This could be explained by the old man swapping out the clocks, or even replacing the hands. Or perhaps I'd misremembered. But it felt like a puzzle made for me.

The next day the clocks changed again. Some were bigger, some smaller, some were a different colour, although all retained elements of their original form. Only the three that kept the right time stayed unchanged.

I decided to leave early the following morning to wait outside the shop. There was a heavy fog when I arrived, and I heard keys jingling before I could see who carried them. A young man was unlocking the door. I thought I'd seen him before, milling around the back of the shop, but I couldn't be sure. I wondered if he remembered me, or if he'd noticed how often I stopped in front of the window. He smiled at me questioningly with one hand on the door handle.

Built-up tension left my body as I uttered one abrupt sentence: 'I want to buy a clock.'

'Sorry,' he said. 'We don't sell those.'

For a moment I thought he was being serious, but then he smiled again.

He took off his puffer jacket and invited me in. The dusty shop immediately dried the fog out of my lungs and I wheezed.

'You'll have to give me a moment,' he said, disappearing through a door. 'Feel free to have a look around.'

The rest of the shop was exactly like the window: five shelves on each wall lined with different kinds of clocks. To the left were the alarms, to the right were some tabletop clocks, while the wall behind the counter was covered top to bottom, with one cuckoo clock hung proudly in the middle. The counter itself was made of glass and showcased a collection of expensive watches.

'Did you change the clocks in the window recently?' I asked through the door.

'I don't think so,' he said, appearing with a cash register. 'Although I only work here part-time so I don't know everything that happens. Did you know what you wanted?'

'I want three,' I said.

He followed me to the window and I pointed at the clocks that had never changed. One was the sleek alarm clock for Daniel, another a standing clock with a small face and a black plastic body, and the third a wall clock with a dark wooden frame.

'Brilliant,' he said, carrying them one by one to the counter, then wrapping them neatly in paper.

'I just moved in around the corner and I have barely anything,' I said, trying to explain my behaviour, but he just smiled again. 'Would the other man who works here know about the changes in the display?'

'If there are any changes he'd know, but I haven't noticed anything.'

After work, I set up the clocks in different parts of the flat; the alarm clock beside my bed, the standing clock on my desk in the corner of the bedroom and the wall clock in the kitchen. This way I could keep an eye on them. I took a photograph of each so I could remember exactly how they looked. Since they had never changed, unlike the others, they were the key to solving the puzzle.

By the afternoon of the second day, the times were already out of sync – the alarm clock falling behind little by little while the other two raged ahead. I started to think the shop was a scam, that there was nothing mysterious at all about their faulty products. Maybe they replaced parts with whatever they had lying around, and that's why the appearances changed.

On the third day, I came back from work and sat at the kitchen table. I looked over at the fridge and tried to imagine what I could cook with the little I had, but something was wrong with the scene.

The clock was gone.

The nail was still there on the wall, but no clock. I ran into my room to find the other two had also vanished. I walked between the rooms three times, checking under the bed and in the cupboards. I put my face right up to my desk in case they had become so small I could no longer see them. They had completely disappeared.

Had they vanished into nothing? Would someone steal clocks but leave everything else? Who even knew they were here, and why would they want them? I thought back to how I'd told the man in the shop I lived around the corner and hurried out of the door, banging it shut behind me.

As I approached the shop, I half expected to see my clocks back in their original places in the window, like guards returned from a reconnaissance mission, but new ones had taken their place.

I opened the door hesitantly, formulating in my head how to ask if they had stolen my clocks without sounding crazy. The old man was speaking to a customer, and it was only when this customer turned around that I recognised him.

'Daniel?'

'Anna! You caught me.'

He put his hands up and chuckled.

'What are you doing?'

'The flight got cancelled so I came back. And I thought I might as well get your clocks fixed while I waited for you. Did you know this place was just around the corner? I guess you did or you wouldn't have found me.'

There was my dissected wall clock laid out on the glass counter. The old man was putting a new piece into it with tweezers. He looked older than I'd realised. He didn't look up at me, as if he knew I was onto him.

'Do you like this?' Daniel asked, holding up his glinting wrist. 'I just bought it. It's a Rolex from the seventies. I couldn't resist it.'

I wanted to sit and calm down, but there were only shelves all around, towering over me. My experiment was ruined. What use were the clocks if they worked perfectly? With the addition of one small piece, they'd be completely different.

The man screwed the back into place and announced he was finished. I saw something strange in his smile.

'Why do you change the clocks in the window?' I asked him.

The cuckoo clock chimed, startling me.

He leaned forward on the counter and studied my face.

'Sometimes we sell the clocks.' He spoke slowly, each word made to linger. 'Is that what you mean?'

I leaned forward against the table too, ready to find a hole in his story. 'You change them around in subtle ways.'

Daniel put his hand on my arm.

'Thanks so much for the work you did on the clocks, we really appreciate it.'

He pulled me back gently.

'You're more than welcome,' the man said.

I snatched the clocks from the counter. They looked the same for now, but who could tell what he had done to them.

On the street, Daniel turned to me.

'What the hell was that about?'

'You're both up to something,' I said.

We didn't even get back to the flat before he announced he was going out drinking with his friends. He thought I had something wrong with me and I needed time to calm down. I found myself sitting on the sofa, drinking red wine and watching the clocks tick until Daniel got back and collapsed on the bed.

When I woke up the next day, I turned over my phone and was startled by the time. It was already midday. I had only one notification – a text from my manager which opened with, 'This is not the first time you've failed to come into work. I'm sorry to say…'

I didn't bother to read the rest.

Why hadn't my alarm clock woken me up? I clearly remembered setting it while Daniel was snoring. I looked over at it, but it was no longer an alarm clock. It was a wall clock lying on its back, ticking loudly. The chrome was replaced by red plastic and it had childlike numbers. I threw it through the doorway and it clattered in the kitchen, but I could still hear it ticking.

I stood up and collected all the clocks into a bin bag. I was about to take Daniel's watch from the bedside table, but then his sleepy, cracked voice said, 'I told you to let me sleep,' and I left it.

I dressed in his uniform, the closest thing I could find to wear, took the bin bag outside and smashed it repeatedly with a brick I'd found by the house. I checked inside the bag. The glass was dust, the metal parts all bent. I emptied it all out bit by bit into different bins along the street, all the way to my work.

I went inside, just like I had thousands of times, and picked up the mannequin. When my manager realised who I was, she rushed towards me.

'Hey! You know you're fired, right? I told you not to come in today. Hey, what are you doing?'

I looked around. The three customers looked up at me, then put their heads down. My one colleague had her head down too.

'Just give up,' my manager said.

I didn't leave until I'd put the mannequin at the back of the store where she belonged.

REVERIE

Jenny Metcalfe

She was rehearsing Debussy. I was polishing the stage door handles. Tin of wax in one hand, my cloth glided with the notes that slid around the almost empty concert hall. Some intern was practising with the spot-lights, once even picking me out – tabard and all – while Aisha vacuumed between the seats in front of the stage. The piano swam above the hoover's sucking groan. Chimes plucked by the pianist's right hand rang through the air; the waves of her left hand eased around the auditorium, massaging the muscles of my arms and back. She repeated bars until they hung like fireflies. When I could see the bulk of the grand piano gilded in the half-moon door handles, I pushed through to backstage, a wheel of my trolley off-key as the door sealed shut behind me. The music muffled, I slid cloth and polish back into their canister and lingered for the next phrase of melody.

The clack of approaching heels was off-beat and syncopated – the over-short stride of someone unused to pencil skirts. The clipboard emerged first, followed by the microphone on a headset. Well, I had a clipboard too, and I busied myself marking off the stage cleaning.

'Sound check in three.'

I didn't think she was talking to me; I wasn't blocking the corridor – no arse is as wide as a procession of cellos. The piano's runs melted into soft, kittenish chords.

'Are you meant to be here?'

I considered the trainee stage-manager while she hooked her biro into the teeth of her clipboard. Every new graduate was much the same as the last.

'There was the children's choir rehearsal this morning.'

'Oh yes, got to scrub away their sticky little prints,' she agreed.

She was about to push through on to the stage when she heard the piano. She rocked back on her heels.

'I'll wait until she's done.'

'Probably for the best,' I placed both hands on my trolley.

'I love Debussy, don't you, Linda?'

New-hires should be made to wear name badges too, whether they are stage-staff or not. I decided to call this one Maud.

'My son played this one all the time,' I said.

'Oh?' Maud just about managed to keep her eyebrows a sensible distance from her eyes. 'Not as well as this, I'm sure.'

I tried to meet her too-bright smile with one of my own.

'He was quite good as a child. His teacher said he was a dreamer – Debussy he could do, Mozart, not as keen.'

'What's he doing now?' She glanced up at the CCTV screen above the door which showed the stage in silent miniature.

'Studying.'

I saw that double-take, Maud, I'm not as old as I look. This is called being work-wearied.

'I love Debussy,' she said. 'But I've never felt his piano work is for a big hall like this. It's for headphones in a dimly lit room, you know?'

She had obviously never let a piece tease its way into her subconscious, see her, until she found herself in the gods, hoover cord pulled too tight and every hair raised, struck as cleanly as if by the hammers on the grand's strings.

'What's your son studying?', she asked. I've heard a concert pianist rehearse the same line for forty minutes while I've scrubbed trumpet spittle from the floor. I know meaning is all in the tone.

'Something useful.'

The pianist dropped into reverberating, low chords. Maud straightened, her face shuttering, and maybe I should have said I don't know what he's studying. He's independent now. He hasn't learned yet that reliance goes both ways. I kicked the brake off the trolley.

'Maybe you should stick around for a concert one evening, you might find you enjoy it,' Maud called after me. Beyond the doors, the pianist leapt into a dance, triplet chords spinning each other round, taunting the earlier darkness.

'Why would I?' I asked, feeling her eyes on the back of my neck. Thirty-five years of emptying bins in rehearsal rooms teaches you that musicians bring their A-game to every note. They're playing to you alone and they know it. A ticket doesn't buy that.

I hummed the Debussy as I worked, sleepwalking through the brushing of resin from black chair cushions until my phone beeped for lunch. Time for a smoke and my first view of the sky in daylight, trapped between the roof of the concert hall and the neighbouring office block. The pianist strode through the performers' exit as I passed towards the kitchens. I paused. She hurried towards the trams. I was feeling person-itched from my encounter with the trainee.

Zoe was reliable as ever, waiting for me in our spot by the heat vent. When we had first met, she had been ankle-deep in soap suds, swearing at one of the chefs about how she had requested a damned technician weeks ago. Over the years, I had come to appreciate her as a constant in a building full of seasonal and university workers. She wouldn't start a loaded dishwasher if the clock said it was time to join me for a fag. She nodded at me as she rolled up and took a long drag. She'd not long had surgery to remove a mole from behind her ear and she had a buzz cut on one side of her head, the only part of Zoe that looked velvet soft.

'Bastards tried to put the hall on again,' she said.

'They don't listen to you.'

I braced myself for another round of Zoe versus the flavour-of-the-day restaurant manager.

'This one thought it would be edifying to watch the rehearsals on the CCTV. They want cutlery for their pre-theatre clientele,' only Zoe could say 'clientele' and make it sound like she was cussing, 'then they can leave the telly alone. If not, I know somewhere to stick their knives.'

Maybe once I would have said something, but after two dozen years of Zoe, I knew a glance would earn me a twitched smile and she would ease back against the glass of the smoking shed, dropping ash on the toe of her boot.

'It was good today,' I said 'should be—'

'Oh don't you start.'

I shrugged. 'Heard her play something Mark used to play.'

Zoe laughed, scrolling on her phone. 'Your Mark's bloody silent, when did he last text you?'

I pretended to check my phone. 'While ago.'

'While ago,' Zoe sucked on her fag, 'he's down where he's got no business being. You lost your grip on him and now he's away.'

'Zoe—'

'Uh uh, I warned you, I said, you're letting him go like you let that scum Liam go, and you let Rick run off with Olivia before that. You don't fight for no man. I used to think that was backbone or pride or something but you'd lick the ground Mark pissed on and now you're getting all teary 'cause some twiglet in heels is playing his music. Jesus, Linz.'

'Zoe.'

She spat into a damp pile of cardboard near the bins.

'He knows I'm proud of him,' I said.

Zoe laughed. 'You told me he's ashamed of you, you told me that.'

The drizzle thickened. I snuffed out my cigarette and reached into my bag for my crisps, tossing them to Zoe. 'I've got nothing to be ashamed of.'

'Did I say that? Let him work for a living, let him get his hands dirty for a change.'

A pianist's hands, all his teachers said so. My own were red and sore, tags of skin peeling back from cracked nails. If he could leap over needing hands like mine, that would be alright by me.

'This is where you belong Linz, hard work but no nonsense, no worrying what anyone else thinks.'

I chewed a mouthful of cheese butty and swallowed.

'He had exams, he'll be back for the summer,' I said, but didn't meet her eye.

Zoe poured crisp crumbs into her palm and licked them up.

'You'll find the sun shines brighter down south, there'll be girls there who don't know he spent his evenings in the mop cupboard, doing his homework with his heels knocking on wet floor signs. He was a good kid, but he's gone now, the kid's gone.'

Zoe glanced at me, tongue worrying at the gaps in her teeth, as if she were digging out old boyfriends, old bosses and old arguments, all chewed up and spat out behind the loading bay. I could never decide whether Zoe was a major or a minor key. In her own way, she was trying to raise me up, like the left hand flying over to the top of the piano.

'No use doubting him before the summer comes,' I said.

Lunch ended, shift ended. Locking the trolley away I struggled with the zip of my handbag, the triplet line of the Reverie flittering around my mind. My keys had fallen into the mess of chocolate wrappers and concert leaflets I carried everywhere. I was shuffling towards the door when it swung towards me and I was caught by a gust of rain. A hand on my shoulder bustled me backwards.

'Do not go outside before you find your keys,' a voice said, half laughing.

It was tonight's pianist, dressed in tight, high-waisted jeans and a Captain America t-shirt. Her concert dress was in a clear plastic bag draped over one shoulder, an iridescent waterfall of sequins and pearls. Sheet music was about to fall from her grip between her elbow and ribs – people need more flesh to carry valuables there – and I lunged forward, sliding the pages loose and shuffling them back into order.

'You're a star,' she said, in a soft American twang. 'I cannot in good conscience let you out into that typhoon now.'

She tried to wipe some of the rainwater off her garment bag. I blew on a couple of pages of the Debussy, where splodges had smudged her pencil marks over the score. I had yet to say a word to her.

'I heard you practise this morning,' I blurted.

'I know,' she said, smiling and reaching out a hand. 'Ying Yue.'

'Linda,' I replied.

Holding her hand was like sandpapering porcelain. She squeezed my fingers.

'You have good rhythm.'

I blinked, smoothing a dog-ear on one of the sheets.

'I, I don't—'

'You polished in time with my playing, I watched you.'

The unexpected heat of being seen bubbled up inside me, steaming my throat and rolling my words from my tongue.

'Oh I'm so sorry, I didn't mean, I didn't want—'

'No! That's not what I'm saying at all,' she said. 'No that's what I want when I play. Have you ever been to the ballet?'

I found myself shaking my head before I could feel stung. The boil was leaving my blood, like a kettle had poured the heat of my embarrassment away.

'Before, well,' she lifted the dress and it shimmered, 'the only paying gig I could find was as a rehearsal pianist for a ballet company. The music didn't sing for me, and morning rehearsals,' she gave a theatrical yawn. 'But then, as my grandma would say, I started paying attention. Even when they warmed up the dancers were listening to me, moving with me, all those gorgeous long limbs in those ridiculous fluffy leg warmers. I would play with the tempo to make them sweat and give them a drum roll before they soared through the air. I was a god, a little god in a little room, but a god nonetheless.'

She was grinning broadly at me, swaying as if she herself were a violin under the bow.

'My son—' I held out her music.

She didn't take it. 'Does he play?'

'He, I don't know if he still does, but he used to.'

'What kind of things?'

'Oh, all sorts, Debussy, but you made me, I mean, I remember one time we were in a pub somewhere up near his nan's and there was a piano. He sat at it, can't have been fifteen, and he played songs I didn't know he knew. Sweet Caroline, Mr Brightside – taking requests from forty-year-old blokes with suit ties shoved in their pockets to duet Queen's '39 – and suddenly the whole pub, we weren't strangers. We were together and singing and shouting what we wanted next and we were dancing. And that was my son. He did that. He did that.'

Ying Yue looked at me, as intense as when she had played the Reverie this morning. 'That sounds god-like.'

'I don't know if he still plays. He's gone to uni and hasn't come to see me in a while,' I said.

She looked at me. It made me want to shiver. She flushed slightly, her teeth worrying at the inside of her cheek.

'Would he – god this is why I don't normally do this – would he know who I am?'

'Yes, I mean, yes I think so. We were here all the time when he was young. He would change the radio to this kind of music at home.'

I gestured at the hall, hoping to wave my hand around all concert music repertoire. She nodded and reached for her scores. She rifled through them, grabbed a stub pencil from her jeans pocket and scrawled something on one of the sheets before handing it back to me.

'Ask him to come home.'

It was Debussy's Reverie. She had signed it.

'But, you, don't you need—'

'Ask him to come home.'

'It's not that simple.'

She placed her hand on my wrist.

'It's only a dream,' YingYue said, 'Anything is possible in dreams.'

I found myself returning her smile and nodding. She saw the time on the clock over my head and swore.

'Got to run. Come say hi next time I'm here, promise?'

'I promise,' I called after her.

I had nothing to carry the music in apart from my crumb-filled bag. I folded the sheets in half, encouraging them to curve rather than bend hoping the fold wouldn't hold. I stepped into the early evening, into the slowing of the day, as the final notes of the Reverie laid themselves down behind my ribs, a rising line from the bass drawing us into a gentle closing chord.

WORDS SPOKEN OVER A BLEEDING WARRIOR

Finlay Worrallo

I do not want revenge because you left me to die. This is war, after all. We have certain obligations and I knew exactly what I was signing up for, all those years ago. I knew I might never see my home again; I knew my life might end at the hands of an enemy; I knew that my end might be as intimate as an act of love. I knew that the last thing I might see could be the eyes of the enemy as I felt his blade. And those eyes turned out to be yours. We battled and you beat me, and I am at peace with that, utterly, utterly. I bear you no ill will for trying to kill me, for that is the law of war. I would have done the same to you.

I want revenge because you changed your mind.

How well do you remember the day? We were up on a cliff overlooking a gorge, on your side of the mountains.

Your patrol had ambushed mine and the two of us were clashing swords. The sunset split the sky, red as my flag, yellow as yours. I remember the thorns scratching my legs as you forced me back, to where the cliff edge crumbled beneath my boots. The sunlight was in my eyes and my strikes were wide. When your sword slashed right across my chest, the wound may not have been deep but the force was enough to thrust me backwards into empty space. And as I fell, you reached out your hands and grabbed onto me – just for a few seconds, long enough for me to feel the dampness of your grip. Long enough for my heart to leap, for my instincts to kick in, for me to grab your arms in return, my thoughts like bright fish leaping from a river – he sees me as a fellow man worthy of life, he has perhaps seen the horror of war, he has perhaps no desire to give up the fight against my people, but cannot bring himself to kill one of us at such close range. Perhaps this is a solitary act of mercy, the kind we make from time to time so we might live with the monsters we have become. But he has chosen to spare me.

All these thoughts flashed through my head – and before I could do more than grasp at your arms, you let me go and I was falling again. Perhaps your grip was looser than I had thought; perhaps your gloves were more slippery with sweat and blood than I realised . . . But that is a lie to comfort us both, and will not serve. Your eyes were the last thing I saw, and I understood the look in them well enough. The shock and repulsion they held was not for me, but for yourself. You had betrayed yourself; you had a moment of such weakness that you had nearly spared the life of an enemy, a heretic, the bastard child of a false god. Nearly. But strength overcame weakness, and now he was falling to certain doom. And I'm sure you can imagine how much more bitter that doom was, knowing how close salvation had been.

Hope is such a vicious master. Have you ever felt it? There is a great freedom in knowing you are about to die and no one can save you, least of all yourself. When I fell the first time, I felt at peace – I had been slain fighting for the dog-headed god, and soon I would be kneeling before Him in person, His breath hot on my lowered head, His great hand on my shoulder. The final seconds of my life were fleeting, snowflakes in my hands, as I hurtled towards holy death. And then you almost saved me, and the hope was like a draught of wine in my veins. The second time I fell, slipping from your hands, the wine turned to poison, and killed any peace within me. I screamed in anguish, and I knew I was not ready to die.

I suppose that is why I did not. I had not died fighting, and so the dog-headed god would not yet welcome me home. Instead of His breath, the next thing I knew was pain. The throbbing of the gash across my chest, the bile in my stomach, the wet twisting of my shin – these things told me I was still alive.

I washed up on the shores of the black river, a day's ride further down the gorge, and for three nights I could do nothing but lie there in the mud beneath the thorn bushes, my hands pressed to my wound. I think hate was the only thing that kept me breathing. I could turn my head and lap at the waters when they were high enough, but other than that I could do nothing more than stare skyward and see your face in the sun and stars. I said that, as you grabbed me, you must have seen me as a fellow being worthy of life – well, it took me a long time to feel the same way in return. At first, I saw you as an anonymous enemy, a heretic born to kill in the name of the cat-headed god. But the longer my bleeding life dragged on, the longer my mind had to rush on like a waterfall that knows no rest. It stripped away your armour and I saw you for who you are. A man, like me. A man of flesh and blood and passion, whose muscles sweat when he works, whose sides ache when he laughs. A man who has known sickness and health, who has loved and lost and given all he has, and who made a vicious choice on that cliff top. If you were a monster, I could forgive you, for what else can a monster be but vicious? Instead, you gave me hope and took it away, and that is worse than anything that your whole murderous army could have done. I saw your naked humanity as I lay in the mud, and I burned for you.

From that moment, I knew the war was over for me. I had died in the War of the Two Gods. You killed me and yet I lived. So I pulled myself out of the mud, washed myself in the river and bound my wounds with reeds. I had to stagger for three days more before I came upon a village. The peasants there gave me food and clean clothes. They let me stay until I was strong enough to set out on firm feet, to fight a second war – but one far smaller, far more intimate than that which I had abandoned. Like a marriage, one against one.

I have searched for you across this entire land, disguised in the browns of the common folk who farm and grow new things. Browns that hide the warrior beneath. I know the greater war rages, still, that your army has not yet won completely, but it is as dead flowers from last springtime for me – ah, I must stop with these expressions from over the mountains. I am sure you will not know them. I doubt that many will, soon. The cities I have crossed to find you have all been conquered. In every square and marketplace, the statues of my god have been beheaded, the cat's head replacing the dog's, again. I have heard that the holy statues have changed heads so many times that nobody knows which came first, dog or cat, much less which one will be the last to survive. But as I said, that war is over for me, and very soon our little war will also be over.

Now I have you. I have tracked you down to your farm, where you have taken off your clothes of yellow and dressed yourself in brown. Neither of us wishes to be a warrior any longer, yet still we must battle. We have fought a second time, and now it is you who bleeds, and it is my hands that are wet and sticky. Are you in pain? I stabbed you well, did I not? Deep enough to kill, but clean enough so that you might hear my story – our story – and hurt as I once hurt.

Look at the stars above us. They draw beasts and heroes in the heavens, and our sweat shines in their light. This is a better place to die, out on the open plains. Better than to fall from a cliff into the mouth of an open gorge. I would leave you here to die alone, but I am wiser than the warrior you let fall. I was wounded, yet I lived – who is to say that you would not survive and come after me again, to stab me once more and leave me to die without hope, only to survive and find you again? We may live out our battle in a great circle, like the cat and the dog swapping heads, like constellations crossing the heavens every night, like lovers bound to the same wheel, to rise and fall and be broken again and again. Who is to say we have not already done so and merely forgotten?

No. I end this war, here. You will die fighting me, and then your goddess will let you into Her gentle halls, to lick your face clean with the tongue that made the mountains rise, to purr over you as you sleep. Thus by your blood is quenched my pain. See my sword shine in the starlight; feel it within you. It will not hurt as much as the hope you gave me. I promise you that.

ROUND TRIP

Vivienne Burgess

I was on the No. 20, just approaching the turn off Shields Road onto Sunderland Road, when my grandad stepped on and flashed his bus pass to the driver. He looked just like he had when I'd last seen him, his smile somehow ancient and juvenile at the same time.

'Eee, what a surprise,' Grandad said, shuffling over. 'Give us a hug then.'

A little taken aback, I moved closer to the window and he lowered himself onto the seat next to me. His moustache was as bushy as ever, white and orange and black like a calico cat. In his hand were a bunch of copper-green coins, ha'pennies and sixpences perhaps. I could almost smell the metallic tang surely staining his palm. Grandad never had gone contactless.

He huffed and groaned as he adjusted himself on the seat. The workman's clothes he was wearing smelled thickly of grease, and he was carrying a little tin bait box, the kind Nana would have packed for him each morning. The oddest part about seeing him like this was the absence of his dog, Rosie. She'd never left his side, the whole time, took to sleeping at the foot of the hospice bed they'd brought into the house. Jumped up at the window and barked when the hearse arrived. My head was so full of questions it was serenely quiet. I looked over my shoulder – no one was paying us any attention.

'Where you off to, then, sweetheart?'

Grandad had already been receiving end-of-life care when I started working at the call centre. I'd only been there a week when mum called to tell me it had happened – he was gone. I went into work the next day but couldn't keep it together. They sent me home on compassionate leave, and I spent the whole bus journey home wishing another passenger would notice I was trying not to cry, just so I could proclaim, 'There's been a death in the family. Someone precious has died.'

'That's nice, love,' he said, absentmindedly. 'Nice to have some pocket money.'

If he was heading to the shipyards, he was going the wrong way. Then again, when work dried up on the river, he had to take any welding job offered, anywhere in the country. It was surreal to imagine him, frail and stooped as I'd known him, hunkered down among the flying orange sparks at his workstation, his milky blue eyes obscured by a welding mask, his body dwarfed by the bellies of sleeping ships.

I'd worn my graduation dress to the funeral; I didn't have the money for a new one. Libby came down the stairs in a tiny black denim skirt and Grandad would have laughed watching Mum trim the frayed edges with the kitchen scissors to make it slightly more appropriate. It was chucking it down the whole day and we all had brown splotches up the back of our legs. Standing about in Nana's living room, I came across one of Grandad's books with a bookmark stuck a third of the way in. On the mantelpiece was his senior citizen bus pass with his little face on it. On the back of the sofa, his flat cap and Rosie's lead. Everyone was looking at each other like they didn't want to be the first one to cry, halfway between giggling and sobbing. The door to the other room was closed. I wondered if the hospice bed had been taken away yet. I didn't open the door to check. I couldn't bear to see it still there, and I couldn't bear to see it gone.

The bus took us past the Boldon fields, where horses wearing raincoats grazed and banners shouted SAVE CLEADON'S GREEN BELT. At the back of the bus, two women who looked so alike they must have been sisters, chatted loudly about what underwear they had on, their blue cornershop bags stretched over cases of cider. We stopped to let on a young mum and her little boy. As they moved down the aisle, he reached and cried out for the Jack Russell on an old woman's lap before his mum pulled him sharply away.

There was a lot of time for thinking on my forty minute commute to the business park. To think about the bland office awaiting me, the uncomfortable chair and the grubby keyboard with the sticky keys. About what funeral directors think when they're walking in front of the hearse. Do they feel guilty when their minds wander? Do they forget they are in the middle of the road? The crematorium was a small red building two minutes from Nana and Grandad's house. They drove us around a bit to make the journey longer. Nana left halfway through the service, we thought she was going to collapse. I had to close my eyes when Dad started his speech, had to squeeze my hands between my thighs, to keep myself from breaking.

Grandad smiled as he looked out the window. The feeble December sun had broken through and was turning the puddles on the pavement into pools of molten steel. He, like my dad after him, had been a natural storyteller. And yet, when I tried to think about it, I couldn't remember anything he told me, only things I was told about him. Other people telling other people's stories. At the shipyard, all the men would have to wait behind a barrier to be let out for the day. Once, just for a laugh, they tied Grandad's loose sleeve to the barrier so when it began to rise, he lifted up as well. At my interview for the call centre, they asked me for an example of going above and beyond to help a colleague and I just kept thinking of Nana insisting he got six feet off the ground and stayed hanging there until everyone came back from lunch.

His wake was full of stories like that. A different pub for every night of the week. Bloody noses after domino games gone awry. Short-lived enthusiasm for raising pigs in the back garden. After the shipyards closed he took a job in France, but felt so homesick after just two weeks, he abandoned his post without telling anyone and ended up on Interpol's missing persons list. Hearing all these stories made me feel lonely, my life so small in comparison. The most exciting part of my day was walking from the bus stop to the business park, ten minutes max. What strange new piece of furniture had appeared in the underpass overnight? A metro thundering overhead. A charm of goldfinches lifting from the overgrown hedges. They always said I'd got my love of animals from him.

'You asked Santy for anything yet?' Grandad asked.

Last year, he and Nana had gifted me a personalised desk calendar, each month accompanied by a grainy photo from summers at the apartment in Corfu. Libby and me in armbands at the waterpark. Nana, impossibly tanned, smoking on the balcony. Grandad, chronically pink, bent over the latest Lee Child hardback we'd squeezed into our over-packed suitcase. Just looking at it I felt the scorch of the midday patio on my feet. The juice from an overripe nectarine running down my wrist. I heard the scuttling of tiny, translucent lizards we chased up the walls. The hum of the air-conditioning all through the night.

The bus was coming up to the roundabout at Harton Nook. Not long now. My mind rushed with all the things I'd meant to ask him, when I'd had the chance. Had he been scared? Did he feel relieved? What had he and the priest talked about when everyone else left the room? Was it like they said, just like slipping away into perfect sleep? It had never felt like the right time to ask him then, and it didn't feel like the right time now.

A gaggle of young boys in dark tracksuits called for the bus to stop, but when it pulled in, one of them just flung an empty pop bottle at the driver's cubicle and they all scattered, laughing and jeering. The driver didn't react, other than to close the doors and pull away. Grandad shot me his familiar grin.

'You going to help your mam with Christmas dinner again? Good lass.'

Grandad had three true loves. Our nana, the footy, and a home cooked meal. The simplest ham and pease-pudding bap was, for him, akin to an eight course banquet at the Roker Hotel. At Christmas he always wanted to put on *It's a Wonderful Life*, and Nana would have a bit too much red wine. Mum would pretend to get all flustered, lighting the pudding on fire. This year he'd asked for my garlic roasted sprouts specifically. None of us were prepared to see his empty place at the table.

Grandad frowned, thinking. 'Will your dad be all by hisself then?'

The bus was swinging into South Shields centre, past the town hall. We were the last two on board. What would happen if I explained why this year had to be different? That he'd already left us. That we were grieving, and every minute roared with his absence. Would he vanish a second time? Would he look at me like I'm mad?

'Mebbe I'll go round then,' he muttered. 'Give him some company…'

I wondered who he was picturing. Was Nana still some bright young thing with a Twiggy hairdo making eyes at him across the bar? Was my dad a toddler or a balding man? Or both? Or neither. I imagined his kaleidoscope memories, faces warped and shifting, a whole life breaking into colour.

The string of red lights afforded us a few more minutes. Grandad's last night in the hospital, we played cards on the little table attached to the hospital bed. We found *thyme* and *syncope* in the crossword. When mum and I first arrived, he said he felt better, which was good, but I'd already clocked the dried blood on his arm from where they'd taken out the drip, which meant he didn't need the medicine anymore, which meant the doctors knew there wasn't any point, which actually wasn't very good at all.

Back at Dad's house after the wake, drunk and sloppy on sugary wine, I stood staring at the large oil painting hanging in the hallway. A footballer in magpie stripes, perched on a fence, dull green fields stretching out behind him. I'd always wondered why Dad had this painting, being a Black Cats supporter and all. 'That's your grandad's grandad,' he said, like it was a throwaway thought. I saw it then, in the eyes, and the footballer's thick, dark moustache. I felt aggrieved. Why didn't anybody tell me before? When I could have asked Grandad about it, about him? For God's sake, why is everybody always waiting until it's too late?

Finally, it was my stop. The last stop. I told Grandad if he just stayed on the bus it would take him all the way back to Durham, past Dad's. But he wasn't listening. He was gazing out the window, following something that had long since vanished and wasn't meant for me. The driver popped open her booth and stepped off for her break, trailing a plume of blueberry smoke. I had to be in my chair and on the phone in five minutes. The time for asking questions was over. Grandad grinned at me, moustache practically up to his eyes. I gave him a quick hug – inhaled his mustiness, felt his solidness – and got off. The driver got back on. I stayed and watched as the bus pulled away, taking him back to the beginning, all the way we had come.

BRINGING HOME

Lauren C. Maltas

Clare was offered tea before she'd even made it through the front door and could ask if she ought to leave her shoes just there, beside a rubbery houseplant. Walking through the hallway, she knew it had been wise to expose the soles of her feet to the coolness of the red quarry tiles. She wanted so much to take off her grey beret, unwrap her scarf, peel away her coat and put her hands, her wrists, her cheeks, onto the stone plinth above the oven. But there was little chance of that with William's mother ushering her on into the living room, telling her to make herself comfortable. Clare wondered by what means she was to make a decision about where to sit, but eventually she took to the green settee. Low to the ground and covered in at least three different stripy throws, it was the one seat next to a coffee table. She'd said no to tea so was bound to be asked if she wanted anything else, and then she would say yes, yes please I'll have a glass of cold water. She would remember to say cold in the hope that it wouldn't just be tap water, or if it was that William's mother would drop an ice cube in there. His mother seemed nice, even if the sort of woman who talks excessively and overly fast when uneasy or sensing unease in someone else. Clare admired her for that and for the pea-green jumper she wore, the letter 'W' woven into it, though she thought it odd to wear such a thick thing in such a stiflingly hot house. Perhaps it wasn't actually so warm, she wondered, perhaps she'd been outside in the cold away from the warmth of a family for too long.

William's mother recounted the story of how she'd learned that there would be an unexpected guest for dinner. Earlier that day, William had asked 'will there be room for another at the table tonight, Ma?'. She'd thought he had plans to go out, but he said he didn't anymore and that was all. 'Of course I asked who it was' his mother said, 'because I've no real options to choose from, no friends' names that pop to the surface. William doesn't talk about anyone anymore, hasn't for a long while. "A friend of mine", is all he said, and that you were having a nightmare of a day.'

Earlier that day a low glass roof had almost fallen onto Clare, missing her by millimetres. She'd stood with her hands on her head, staring down at the scattered shards on the floor around her until a railway operator got her attention, shaking her at the elbow. He got her a cup of tea at the platform's Pumpkin Café and made her sit on one of those clinical metal benches that suck the warmth from your thighs. He bumbled on about how lucky she'd been and asked if there were any small shards caught in her hair or in her hat, did Clare want him to have a look, could he call anyone to collect her. Clare thought about phoning her manager, this was a work trip after all, but she decided against it almost immediately. She'd rather call no-one than call a colleague who was certainly not a friend. It occurred to her then to phone William, who she was meant to be meeting for dinner that evening, something he'd suggested when she'd told him she was staying over his way for work and mentioned she didn't really know the area. He'd seemed really pleased that she was coming, even though they weren't all that close. She would have described them as somewhere beyond acquaintances but wasn't all that sure what came next, stunted by an expanse between them. As she scrolled through her contacts to find his number, she realised this wasn't something she'd ever done, that they'd only sent a few messages and met up as many times in person. He was surprisingly easy to talk to on the phone though, she knew it right from the moment he picked up with a 'Hey Clare! Everything all right?'. All she'd planned to say was that she'd been in a bit of an accident and might be a little late getting to his neck of the woods – would he be able to shift their dinner later or cancel it? 'Actually, cancelling it might be best, I'm not exactly sure what time I'll be getting in now.' He asked her what had happened and if she was OK, and that was when she began to say, 'Well, it's not as if I was actually in an accident, I was on the edges of it, just on the periphery really.' She was going to say 'like a bystander' but somehow that wasn't quite the word for it and she felt she wouldn't have known that without having had it pulled out of her by this phone call. She told him she was fine, 'more than fine! And don't worry.' It was then that he'd asked her to have dinner at his house with his family instead, he'd even offered to come and pick her up even though she was still silly miles away, and there was something about it that seemed to warm the paper cup of cold tea that had been idling between her legs the whole time.

Dinner would be ready shortly, William's mother said, as she made her way back into the room from the kitchen, a small grey cat slinking in behind her. While she'd been gone, William had reduced his voice to a whisper. 'I hope you're hungry,' he said. 'She's made loads. If she'd known you were coming, she'd probably have baked a cake too.' Though Clare smiled at William's attempt to put her at ease, it struck her as strange that his mother didn't sit back in the seat she'd previously occupied, instead leaning on the arm of William's chair and staring down at the top of his head.

William started to say something about how long Clare's journey must have been, and it was then that the cat jumped up onto the settee next to Clare, trampling over the coat she'd peeled off before it settled next to her and began to knead its claws into her thigh. Clare stroked the cat from the top of its head down the length of its spine and they developed something of a rhythm, like the chain and pedals propelling the wheels of a bicycle. William's gaze had become foggy as if his thoughts were elsewhere, deep in a memory of another time, and Clare wanted a glimpse of it. She'd seen photographs of a small boy lying down like a cat on his grandmother's sofa, his head on her lap, and wondered what it would be like to be there. She imagined their talks about growing up, William learning to oil the chains on the bikes, shave his face without injury. An old man in the scene would put whiskey in his coffee and tell William that one day he'd have a nice wife. A wife who would be good with the animals, who would need him to fill up a hot water bottle, and tuck it into their bed every night in the winter.

Clare was pulled back to the room when William's mother stood up and declared that dinner was ready, and that even if it wasn't, she couldn't wait any longer. The moment she'd disappeared back into the kitchen,

William's father entered the room as if he'd been lying in wait.

'How lovely to meet you, Clare!' he said, as William introduced them, his father removing his glasses and slotting them smoothly into the breast pocket of his waistcoat. 'And to know your name, finally, too. All day I've been calling you "the girl that William is bringing home", haven't I, Love?' In the kitchen, William's mother didn't answer the question, instead she called out 'Come! Let's eat!'

The meal itself was pleasant enough. Clare managed to survive William's father's fishing-expedition, though she wished she'd thought of something better to say than 'Yes, in a way,' when he'd asked if she had family. He'd laughed and replied, 'Well, surely that's a simple question to answer, no?' All she could do was smile weakly and gulp down the remains of the lukewarm summer fruits cordial she'd been given, while the others at the table consumed greedy mouthfuls of dry roast potatoes.

When William's mother dropped a serving dish to the floor on the way to the sink, Clare almost jumped out of her seat, the old memory it stirred rising up her throat like a sick feeling. Knowing that the best way to calm herself was to focus on the source of the unease, she stared at the disparate pieces of porcelain while William's parents scurried around them. But the sick feeling rose further, and the porcelain pieces lost all pigment for Clare, first becoming the shards of glass that had surrounded her at the train station earlier that day, and then the shards from her mother's cheap coffee table, the one that twelve-year-old Clare had shattered with the TV remote when her mother had bounded in and made her move. It had made no difference to her mother's stony face when Clare pleaded 'But I watch TV between six and seven, that's the rules!' All her mother said was 'Not today. Simple as that' and draped her legs like a heavy coat over the settee's arm. It was the calmness of the response that Clare remembered most vividly, the way her rage had been made insignificant by the lack of raised voices that followed the sound of glass smashing, by the lack of a dash to the cupboard for the dust pan and brush. As the sick feeling subsided, Clare could see both things at once; the glass and the porcelain, the simple and the not.

After dinner, Clare said no thanks to coffee, saying that she would be on her way and thanking them for their hospitality. William offered to drive her and said he'd fetch her coat and hat from the sitting room, but returned with only the coat. 'I'm sorry but the cat's asleep on your hat,' he said, 'she'll scratch my eyes out if I try to get at it.' There was silence for a few seconds, something about it felt to Clare like a fresh breeze coming in through a window she'd thought jammed.

'No problem,' she said, 'I don't need it. Don't bother the cat.'

In the car the silence between them was broken when William asked Clare if the blower was too hot or not hot enough, and commented on why he was driving to her hotel this way, rather than the way she'd probably come in the taxi from the station, though she could hardly tell the difference in the darkness. He explained the historical significance of this bridge and that building, and that the butchers over there bore his family's name because it was his great-uncle's. Without the hat, Clare found she was a bit chilly but it was a relief after being too hot all evening. She began to think about whether or not she'd have felt hot or cold had that glass fallen directly onto her, would the heat from the blood rushing to the surface have outweighed the coolness of the shock. As they sped past a crowd of children, all vying for the attention of a woman who had a phone in one hand and a cigarette in the other, Clare put her hands to her cheeks and said, 'It's a joke really, isn't it. Unbelievable.' William said nothing, though she sensed that his grip of the steering wheel had tightened. As they turned the corner onto the street where Clare's hotel was, he slowed the car and turned down the already quiet stereo. 'Look Clare, I'm sorry. I don't quite know what you want me to say. I'll get the hat back to you as soon as possible.'

UNDER RED LIGHT

Rory Thorp

Laugh along with the girls even though they're laughing at you. Hide behind your smile as your insides twist like knotted rope. At the first opportunity, excuse yourself and negotiate safe passage down the spiral staircase, clinging onto the clammy wooden banister. Avoid the server's parting glance and wander out of the coffeeshop.

On the street, hug the wall so the girls can't see you. The world feels soft on your eyes and is coloured a hazy gold by old-fashioned street lights. Bikes float past in your peripheral vision and bricks graze your fingers but there's no blood. Stop on a street corner. Hide your burning cheeks and your swollen eyelids. Wait for the world to still.

Admit this was inevitable. The prosecco and the idea of escaping your stiflingly conventional parents blinded you. A weekend with the girls is probably worse than home. Although, on the first night, there was one radiant moment when you ran through Amsterdam Centraal and out to the river, your mum's pink suitcase clicking like a miniature, caffeinated steam train. The night was cool and new and you felt you could pull all that air into your lungs and it'd propel you up and up until you strained against the clouds. But the girls caught you and asked whether you'd shag this footballer on Dutch Tinder.

Remember Amsterdam is only east of Norwich.

Put your black curls into a bobble to take the sticky heat from your neck. Continue away from the girls, keeping your head down. Focus on square belt buckles, stonewash jeans, dark brown or orange skirts, coupled hands swinging. Try not to cringe when you pass the sex shops with their leather masks, ball gags and fluorescent dildos, otherwise people will look and laugh again.

The girls will message you later. They are used to you taking a walk. Whether that be when they make a harsh joke or that deep part of the night when lads try their shocking lines and the girls titter because they want to be taken home.

You find yourself inside Dam Square with its pointy church and relentlessly square buildings. You take a seat on a cold stone bench. Everyone you see is part of a couple other than a wizened man with pigeons perched on his shoulders. He's wearing a shabby overcoat, but he's grinning. A glamorous couple stab their fingers at him and joke between themselves. You smile along with the man, but, when the couple sees you, you look down.

Feel your cheeks with red hands. They're no longer throbbing hot so maybe you look normal. You remember the coffeeshop, how the girls cackled and spluttered smoke, their eyes piercing through the grey haze like glinting knives. How your cheeks seared and the air grew thinner with each shallow breath. You stared at the TV as it played 'Losing My Religion'. You wished you were the man alone in the music video dancing as if no one was watching. It all came from Tash: a joke. That they couldn't even buy you a boyfriend.

Take out the silly hoop earrings and fake eyelashes they made you wear. They can never be yours and you don't want them to be. Store them deep in the pocket of your jeans. Set off in search of more weed so you don't have to think about going back.

You see a neon marijuana leaf buzzing on a street corner. Take the three steps down and ease the door open. Inside is dark as stout. Languid music thumps on your chest while men in booths mumble like gangsters. Once at the bar, make yourself small, and wait for the server with the handlebar moustache to stop talking to another customer.

His look skewers you, but don't let it show. Wait for him to say, I didn't see you, in accented English, before you point out the strain Wide Awake on the sticky, warped menu. Ask for it pre-rolled because you never learned how. You didn't want to become dependent. You've always struggled to say no to easy, anonymous time away from real life.

Having a good time? a guy down the bar asks while Handlebars is looking through his trays. The girls would call him fit. He has a sharp jaw and slicked-back blond hair and he's wearing those black and white classic Vans every fuckboy owns. Take your time turning so he knows you don't want this. Great, thanks. His eyes are red and heavy. He stares at the smoke rising from his joint and you know what's coming from nights out with the girls. Do you like pizza? he says. My hotel does great pizza. He smiles like a dog with a secret. Trust me, you'd love it. You wonder whether it's a nightmare, but no one else is watching. Say, sorry, my boyfriend's outside, pay for your joint, and escape.

The sky is an inky black that all the streetlights can't reach. There are no stars, but, as you walk, you notice there are more people, more couples. Everywhere you look, you feel like an intruder, peeping smiles that don't belong to you.

When your leg buzzes, you pull out your phone. Zoey says it was only a joke. When are you coming back? And that took her an hour. You receive another message from Tash that says, get over yourself. Stare at it like an open wound. Put your phone away. Keep walking. You try to steady your shaking legs but it's like stacking water.

The street opens out into a square that is spotlight-bright in its centre. Establishments blaring with garish neon line the edges, eyeing you, and a statue of Rembrandt lords over the men from *The Night Watch*. Some tourists take pictures but most cluster around something else. Dissolve into the crowd and feel your heart begin to steady. Take in the smell of glittery perfume and sweet booze from the woman beside you. Sneak glimpses of the line of her teeth above her scarf, her maroon nails when she tucks a strand of hair behind her ear.

Tinny, swooning music starts to play and the crowd quietens. A busker starts singing 'A Whole New World'. His voice cracks, making you wince, but he beams as he glides around the square, serenading his audience. They watch with cruel curiosity – as if waiting for a server's stack of plates to topple – and you glimpse a gang of lads further down erupt into hissing laughter. The maroon-nailed woman whispers into a man's ear and he grins, rests his hand on the small of her back. Your stomach is in knots.

The busker finishes and the crowd claps as it should. You clap with them and not a moment after. He thanks everyone and his accent is so American-college educated it hurts. He gestures to an upturned flat cap and says, any patronage is very welcome. You hope he doesn't actually wear the cap, that it's only an unorthodox piggy bank. His polka-dot suspenders are bad enough. A few people flick him change, and he thanks them, his smile resolute, as those lads snigger and shoot him with their phone flashes on.

When he starts to sing 'I'll Make a Man Out of You', you notice the line of placid smokers at the edge of the square. You find shelter beneath a tree and light your joint, the busker pulling everyone's attention. The tip brightens and crackles. As you puff, the cool air on your skin becomes heavier but gentler. The crowd fidgets and starts to mutter as they watch him. Some shake their heads and leave, trying to ignore his existence.

As he finishes with a tortured flourish, stub out your joint, and approach the centre of the square. Sidle through bodies as applause patters through the crowd. Have your change ready. He turns to you, bows, and grins like he alone knows how to fly. Much appreciated, madam. When you're in the centre, with all those eyes choking you, his unceasing smile becomes miraculous rather than crazy. You manage to smile back until he turns away and you stride out of the square as if on an airport runway, gaining momentum.

The red brick streets are bright with immaculate light and you strut as if every step takes you further into the sky. Cloud-cool air brushes your skin, and the corners of your mouth curl up. You meet the eyes of others and smile at the woman in the tight white jeans. You're heading where you need to go and you're unstoppable.

The pockets of walkers aggregate into a thick crowd, their chatter a buzzing mass in your chest. Diffuse light turns the crowd and canal misty red. Try to ignore the growing black hole in your belly. You're going to do this.

The girls would never believe you could.

Follow the slow tide into De Wallen. Couples, singles and families mill around as if it's the Christmas markets and they're perusing mulled wine and mini-pancakes in the glowing red windows. The district smells of cigarettes and the human scent of others: either fragrance or sweat. You clutch the canal railing and catch glimpses of the women through the crowd. They're insanely beautiful, ageless underwear models preserved in blocks of strawberry ice, and you wonder whether it's their defiant smirks under all those hungry eyes that make them glow.

Your phone rings and you flinch as if your mum is knocking on your bedroom door. The synthetic light brands the back of your eyes. Zoey. You stop beside the canal and your body is leaden with the idea of explaining yourself. They'll drag you back to the apartment, and maybe they won't say anything to start with, but they will make fun of you. They'll call you crazy and laugh with their eyes because they don't understand a thing.

Decline the call and turn the phone off.

Relight your joint with trembling hands. Smoke to calm your thudding heart and melt the metal in your jaw. The canal is glassy and striped with orange light. Focus on this rather than the human flow around you that thrums like a bug zapper.

Crush the joint into a cigarette bin and submerge yourself into the flow. Try to look past the hungry smiles to find something real. Slow when you see a woman with a tattoo of a snake coiled around her thigh with a black flower crown on its head. Her pale body is covered in silver piercings and her nose is too big to be conventionally pretty. You watch as men walk past, ignoring her calls. Sometimes they nudge each other and laugh, but she only smirks to herself. She simply moves on, untouched, and calls out again.

Stride out of the flow and into the red light. She sees you and rises. Her mouth cuts into a smile and she opens the door far enough for it to slam. The heady warmth from inside caresses your skin like a close breath. Hi, baby, you are beautiful, she says with a husky, Slavic accent, and you're struck by the fact no one has ever said that to you, and that people should say it more often because it costs nothing. Do you want good time? she asks. Nod. 50 euros. Hand it over straight away so you can't run.

She opens the door and you're pulled through the red tunnel into the next room, your mind working like an obscene flipbook. The door clicks shut and the world holds its breath. The smell of red flowers muddies your head as she leads you deeper into a room dense with light the colour of flesh. As you stare at the black leather bed, she puts a grasping hand around your waist, sending tremors into your throat. Sit, she says, comfortable, yes? Force a smile as she passes close to you, leaving behind a fragrant fist of metal stars.

The black leather groans under you. You watch as she squats and roots through a huge handbag in the corner of the room. Her black hair is tied up leaving only a few tendrils curling down her slender neck. As prickly warmth floods your body, count the bumps of her spine, and when she finds what she's looking for – a pair of thin black gloves she might use to commit murder – try to relax your zipped-up legs.

You'll open them to a stranger in minutes. That's the whole point.

The latex fidgets as she pulls on her gloves. You stare at her flexing fingers, each one popping and clawing. She turns and approaches, the room thick with silence. You're submerged so deep in your head that your lungs burn. She lifts your chin with a soft, hooked finger, cradles you with her inhuman eyes, and you hear the small sounds of her mouth. Relax, she says, I do a lot. A smile softens her face and you grin.

She takes the zip of your jacket and begins to pull down and, with that steady purr, it's like she's peeling away an outer skin you never needed. A cork pops inside you and new year champagne fizzes down your skin. Your body hums with sweet vibration and you want to bathe in that crackling euphoria, growing lighter and lighter, forever.

Then her breasts are in your face and she's prying your shirt from your jeans with mechanical efficiency. You want her to stop because you're not done with that last moment, but she continues doggedly, her eyes lost to the mundane task, and you're left with a stranger, in a foreign room, trying to make ends meet. She doesn't even know your name.

You place your hands on her ribs, staring at her undulating belly button stud, and ease her backwards. Thanks, you say, but I'm going to leave now. She puts her hands on her hips. No refund. That's fine, you say. Her face gives you nothing. You hope she isn't hurt.

You grab your jacket and pull it on. You smile and she gives a thin smile back before you ease open the curtain and the door and step outside. All the wide-eyed stares evaporate on your smouldering skin. It only takes a few seconds back in the human flow – chafing against the crowd's rhythm – before you have to break out.

Anchored by the canal railing, you notice a red light blink out across the water. You stare, waiting for it to turn back on, and you're still waiting when you think of De Wallen during the daytime. The fronts are faded brown or dusty grey, the brick walkways visible and gaping, and every window is empty. All the lights will fall to nothing, eventually, and this night will drain away the same as any other. You keep staring. You wish for the red light.

Contributor Biographies

ISABELLA SHARP

Isabella Sharp is a prose writer who lived in the North until April 2023 – since then, she's moved to London for her career. She enjoys writing about women and her favourite authors include Kate Elizabeth Russell and Elena Ferrante. She is currently seeking agency representation for her novel Girls Who Disappear.
isabellasharp98@gmail.com

EMILY YATES

Emily Yates is a prose writer from Manchester. Her first two novels were YA fantasy, and her most recent work is autofiction. Her story in this anthology is her first piece to be published, although she has had a story commissioned by Leeds 2023. She is reading English Language and Literature at Oxford University.
X: @emilycharlyates

ALICE NOEL

From Norwich, Alice is a prose writer of both long and short fiction. In 2017, her short story 'Behind These Eyes' was longlisted in Storgy's Shallow Creek competition and published in the Shallow Creek anthology. After completing her MA in Creative Writing at Lancaster University, Alice now lives and works in Oxford.

JAMES VARNEY

James Varney is a writer, facilitator and theatremaker based in Manchester. He has delivered programmes of workshops for Manchester International Festival, Manchester Literature Festival, First Story, and Bolton Libraries. James's recent theatre work includes Prince Gorge, a narrative poem performed with a live band. He is currently working on a novel, Animals Without Backbones, in which a city's waterways fill with living, hungry flesh.

X: @mrjvarney

BETH LEE

Beth Lee is a writer, graphic designer and artist from Lincolnshire, now living in Vienna, Austria. She studied Fine Art and Creative Writing at Lancaster University, and is just finishing a masters in Graphic Design from Falmouth University while working as a graphic designer. Her writing focuses on prose which straddles the boundary between everyday life and the surreal and fantastical.

Contact: bethanyjane_lee@yahoo.co.uk

JENNY METCALFE

Jenny Metcalfe writes in the early mornings before being called to her day job. Currently working on a novel where the distinction between history and lies is blurred, the only thing she has been doing longer than writing is playing the piano. She hopes to develop the inspiration from her favourite piano pieces into a short story collection about people who – in one way or another – find themselves haunted by reverberating chords and dancing keys.

FINLAY WORRALLO

Finlay Worrallo writes poetry, prose and scripts, and regularly experiments in the spaces in between. He studies Modern Languages at the University of Newcastle. His work is published in *VIBE*, *Queerlings*, *14*, the Braag's speculative fiction chapbook *Unfurl: Portrait of Another World*, and the Emma Press' anthology *Dragons of the Prime: Poems about Dinosaurs*.

Instagram: X @fworrallo

VIVIENNE BURGESS

Vivienne takes a lot of bus journeys. She lives by the North Sea with her elderly cat, Tuppence. She is active on Instagram at @dibsonraoul where she keeps 'watching' and 'reading' highlights.

LAUREN C. MALTAS

Lauren C. Maltas is a writer based in Calderdale, West Yorkshire. She writes fiction and essays on themes including memory, queerness, the past and future. In 2022, her work-in-progress novel 'Perseverance' was awarded second place in the Writers & Artists Working Class Writer's Prize.

X @laurenCmaltas

RORY THORP

Rory Thorp is a writer based in Widnes, Cheshire who specialises in literary short fiction. His writing mainly explores masculinity, desire, and the search for intimacy. He is working towards his first collection of short stories.

X @rory_thorp

Acknowledgements

Many thanks to the following people who have helped bring this anthology together, generously lending their time and expertise:

Marigold Atkey is Publisher at Daunt Books.

Emma Ewbank is a designer who has worked in the publishing industry for over 15 years. The companies she has worked in-house for include: HarperCollins, Simon & Schuster, Penguin and Bloomsbury. She now works freelance, and can be found at: www.emmaewbank.com

Madeleine Feeny is the fiction previewer at *The Bookseller* and a freelance literary critic published in *The Times*, *New York Times*, *Guardian*, *Financial Times* and *Economist*, among others.

Katie McLean (she/her) is a freelance publishing professional offering editorial and design services. Her recent projects include *Northern Dreaming* (LEEDS

2023 and the British Library, 2023). Her debut middle-grade novel was shortlisted for the Guppy Books Open Submission 2023 and is currently longlisted for Undiscovered Voices 2024.

Lauren Whybrow is an editor at Bloomsbury Publishing and a writer published in various non-fiction books.

Many thanks also to Libby Williamson and Billie Collins, whose help was essential throughout the process, Laura Jones-Rivera for the typesetting template, and, as always, to Steve Dearden for being the engine behind everything.